A Boy of Tache

by Ann Blades

Tundra Books

It is spring. The long winter is over at last, and at the Indian reserve of Tache in northern British Columbia, the time for trapping beaver is here. The men of Tache are getting their riverboats ready. As soon as the ice goes, they will set out.

Charlie is excited. Today his grandfather Za told him, "With a strong wind, in couple of days, maybe the ice will be no more."

Every day Charlie gets up at six o'clock, and runs down to Stuart Lake. Then one morning he sees what he has been waiting for. The wind has blown the ice away from the shore, piling it up on a rock in the middle of the lake. Big spaces of bright blue appear, and by afternoon only half of the lake is covered by ice. Charlie knows that tomorrow they will go trapping.

Early the next morning, Charlie and his grandparents carry their supplies to the riverboat. They take barrels of gasoline, beaver traps, life jackets, blankets, sugar, salt, flour, tea, dried moose meat, a hunting knife, and a rifle.

Soon the stillness of the morning is broken by the noise of the outboard motor. Charlie listens to the water slapping the sides of the boat, and watches the village. He sees his brothers chopping wood, and his sisters carrying buckets of lake water into the house. The children look up and wave at Charlie. Charlie, the lucky one. His eleven brothers and sisters are busy with chores, and Charlie is going to trap beaver.

Charlie is glad that he was chosen to live with Za and Virginia. During the winter he works hard for them — getting firewood with his sleigh, checking the rabbit trapline, breaking ice on the lake and carrying water to the house. But now spring is here and it is trapping time! Charlie knows how lucky he is, and he feels content.

As the boat speeds past the village, Charlie notices other people getting ready to set out in boats. He sees Alec Pierre on his horse. Alec's rifle is strapped to his saddle, so Charlie knows that he is hunting beaver too.

When Za, Virginia and Charlie reach the mouth of the Tache River, Za stands up and looks around. Ice has piled up at the river mouth. The river is low, but free of ice. Za continues to watch the river closely, and steers the riverboat into the deepest channel. There are white markers at the river's edge to show the safest route, but Za doesn't look at them.

Za has used this river for over fifty years, and he knows it well. Some people run aground in the Tache River, and hurt their boats. But not Za. Many times he has traveled this river at night in complete darkness. Za jokes that he could take a boat up the river with his eyes closed, and Charlie believes him. Charlie watches every turn in the river. He wants to know the river too, so that in a few years, he will be able to work as a guide.

Charlie is still thinking about the old man when they reach Trembleur Lake. They are very lucky. Ice covers half the lake, but there is enough room for Za to take the boat around it, close to the shore. Charlie looks at Trembleur Lake and thinks of the warm summer days he will spend here with Za and Virginia, picking berries and fishing. Charlie imagines himself swimming in the lake while Za sets out the nets and Virginia dries the fish in the sun. Summer is Charlie's favorite time, and he can hardly wait!

Soon Za, Virginia and Charlie pass a hunting lodge on the shore of Trembleur Lake. Charlie's father works as a guide for the hunters and fishermen who come here in the spring, summer and fall. Someday Charlie wants to guide here, just like his father.

Just past the lodge, Charlie and his grandparents reach the mouth of the Middle River, and Middle River Village. Za steers the boat towards the shore, and Charlie jumps out to bring it to a stop against the wharf.

As they tie the boat and walk towards the cabins, Charlie looks at the people standing in the doorways, and realizes that most of them are from his village. They are here to trap beaver too.

Charlie smiles at old Camille, who lives in Middle River Village all year. "Hadé, Charlie. Soointo?" Charlie speaks to Camille in the Carrier language he has learned from Za and Virginia. Camille tells Charlie to learn all about trapping from Za. "When you grow older," he says, "you will trap as many beaver as Za."

Charlie listens to what the men are telling Za. There is still a little snow on the ground. They have many beaver. It is a good year. The price is good for beaver now.

It is late afternoon when Za, Virginia and Charlie get into their boat once more and head up Middle River.

Again Charlie watches the river closely. He sees an eagle circling high overhead. The eagle swoops low, and Charlie watches him. What a beautiful, powerful bird! Za is watching too. "Not many left now," he says. "Long ago he was all over. Now we see one, maybe two."

At dusk, Charlie and his grandparents reach their cabin. Charlie and Virginia carry the supplies inside while Za lights a fire in the wood stove. Then they eat a bit of dried moose and drink some tea. Za and Virginia sleep on the bed, and Charlie curls up under a blanket on the floor.

The next day, Za and Charlie set their traps along the river. It takes them a long time to walk through the trees and brush. They return to the cabin in the afternoon. Virginia has baked some bannock — a kind of bread that Charlie loves. They have a good supper, and go to bed when the sun sets.

Every day Charlie and Za check the traps. The first day there is nothing. The second day there is one beaver in a trap. On the way back to the cabin Za suddenly stops Charlie and points to the river. About a yard from the river's edge, Charlie sees a beaver swimming towards the shore. The beaver climbs up on the land, and Za says, "That beaver will have a baby soon. We will leave that one alone."

The next morning, Za and Charlie decide to go inland for a few days. They take the rifle, some blankets and a bit of food. They walk all morning. They stop only for a short rest whenever Charlie gets very tired. In the late afternoon, Charlie shoots a grouse. Za builds a fire while Charlie cleans the bird, and then they roast it on a stick over the fire and eat it in their hands.

That night Charlie and Za cut cedar boughs, and make a bed under a big tree. There is still snow on the ground, so they pile the boughs thickly to keep warm. Charlie awakes early the next morning. He is shivering, and Za looks cold too.

Za tells Charlie that they will head back to the cabin today. Za says he is getting a cold sick, and he has to be careful. He is an old man — seventy-four years old, and not as strong as Charlie.

They walk all day, very slowly, and reach the cabin at night. Za falls onto the hard bed and goes to sleep. Virginia can tell that her husband is very sick.

"Charlie, you go for bark," Virginia says. Charlie has done this once before. He gets the balsam bark, the spruce bark, the rock plant and the branch of the cranberry tree. Virginia asks Charlie to get two more things and then that is all she needs. Virginia puts the bark in a pan of water and boils it over the stove for a long time.

Charlie watches the steam from the pan. He gets up to bring in more wood. He looks at Virginia. He knows that she is worried, even though she says nothing. Charlie listens to Za's heavy breathing, and wonders if this will be his last cold sick.

Virginia lifts Za's head and makes him drink the brew when it is ready. Then Za sleeps, and Charlie and Virginia watch him, and listen to his breathing get worse and worse.

"Maybe he is getting pneumonia, Charlie." Virginia sounds scared. She knows that Za might die if he gets pneumonia now.

The next morning, Charlie and Virginia are still awake, still watching Za. Virginia gives Za the brew of the bark during the day, but his cold gets worse.

Charlie keeps bringing in wood to keep the stove going. The cabin must stay warm for Za. That day Za doesn't wake up. He tosses on the bed, and moans in his sleep. He throws off his blanket. His head is wet, and Virginia keeps wiping it dry so Za won't get a chill.

Three days later Za still has his cold sick. Virginia knows that he is dying. Her brew of bark has not cured him. Za is too old and too weak to have the strength to get well. Virginia knows that they must get Za to a doctor, or he will die. Virginia has seen many babies die of pneumonia. She knows that Za is near death.

"Charlie, you must go. I will stay with Za. You go to Camille. Get help."

Charlie goes to the riverboat and starts the engine. The boat moves swiftly, moving with the current. Charlie is very careful. If he touches the river bottom, if he hits a log, he won't be able to get help. He thinks of only one thing. "Get to Camille as fast as you can."

In about an hour, Charlie reaches Middle River Village and Camille. He ties the boat up and runs to the house. Camille is repairing the smokehouse. "Camille, Za has a bad cold sick. He needs help. Virginia thinks he's got pneumonia."

Camille goes with Charlie to the boat, and heads around the edge of Trembleur Lake. He knows Virginia. If she says Za is sick, he must be very, very sick.

It seems like hours later when they reach the beginning of the Tache River, and start down its winding course. Charlie is scared. "What if we can't get help? What if they think Za isn't really sick?"

Finally they reach the camp, and Camille and Charlie run up to the trailers. Camille asks to use the radio phone. Charlie listens as the phone rings at the other end and Mel answers. Camille tells him about Za's cold sick: "We need a plane. You can land on Middle River near Za's cabin. Over." "Good. We'll be there right away. Northern Airways off."

"Well, Charlie, we go to Middle River quick," Camille says. They get in the boat, and go straight back to the cabin. Virginia is very glad to see them. Za is worse. He doesn't have much time, they all know. They sit in silence, waiting for the sound of the plane. Charlie thinks he hears it and runs outside, but it was just his imagination.

Then suddenly Camille says "That's it." They can all hear it now. They run outside to watch the plane approach.

It lands safely and Charlie and Virginia watch as Za is helped onto the plane. The pilot starts the motor and the plane takes off.

Charlie and Camille watch as the plane gets smaller and smaller.

Camille turns to Charlie. "Za will get better, Charlie. He never gives up. But this will be his last trip. You will hunt and trap for Za and Virginia now. I know you can do it, Charlie."

Tache, British Columbia

The community of Tache on Stuart Lake, B.C. is located on the site of the old aboriginal village of Thatce. The present-day Tl'azt'en Nation was once known as the Stuart Trembleur Band. Tl'azt'enne (members of Tl'azt'en Nation) belong to the Carrier family of the ancient Déné tribes of northern British Columbia and North America. Tache is parallel with the southern tip of Alaska, some 200 miles inland from the Pacific coast.

It is interesting to compare the picture of Tache life in Ann Blades' book with the first detailed published account of the Carrier Indians of Stuart Lake. During the 1880's Father A.G. Morice, O.M.I., actually lived at Thatce. He was particularly impressed with the intelligence, skills, and energy of the people. They not only learned new techniques of building very quickly, but, he writes, "their homes are just as well built, and often quite as comfortable, as those of any white man who ever ventured in their country. They possess horses and cattle, which they keep in stables and feed at the cost of much personal exertion during their long winters. Close by their habitations, some of them have regular carpenter shops, wherein they turn out such difficult work as window sashes, fancy boxes, etc., while a number boast the possession of sleighs, cutters, and pack saddles of their own manufacture." (Today many Tache residents work on construction jobs and in logging camps in the area.)

According to Father Morice there was very little fur hunting done before the arrival of the fur trader, "save what was indispensable to the family's subsistence and clothing." Afterward beaver hunting became a major source of income for the community, and was pursued both during the winter months and as soon as the ice left the lakes. Father Morice describes a variety of methods used in the beaver hunt — harpooning, trapping, netting, "besides occasional shooting," all of them based on intensive observation and knowledge of the animal's behavior.

The white birches that figure so prominently in Ann Blades' illustrations seems always to have been important to Carrier life. Not only was the bark used for canoes and medicinal purposes but — to Father Morice's amazement — "they employed it in making vessels or dishes of any size and shape. One kind, remarkable for the absence of any seam (the bark being simply folded on its four corners and so retained by a split encircling switch) did service as a kettle or boiler." It boiled liquids very rapidly, but "they had to keep it away from the flames."

One poignant fact emerges from Father Morice's descriptions. He reports that in the 1800's the Tache residents numbered 1,600. A century earlier, when Alexander Mackenzie entered the territory, it is estimated to have been ten times that number. When Ann Blades taught at the two-room schoolhouse there in 1969, the village numbered about 300.

References:

Morice, Father A.G. "The Western Dénés: Their Manners and Customs," paper published in the Proceedings of the Canadian Institute, 1888-1889.

Morice, Father A.G. "Are the Carrier Sociology and Mythology Indigenous or Exotic?" paper published by the Transactions of the Royal Society of Canada, Section II, 1892.

Published in Canada by Tundra Books, Montreal, Quebec H3Z 2N2
and in the United States by Tundra Books of Northern New York, Plattsburgh, New York 12901

Library of Congress Catalog Number: 94-62178

Canadian Cataloging in Publication Data

Blades, Ann, 1947-

   A Boy of Tache

ISBN 0-88776-350-2

   I. Title.
PS8553.L33B6 1995   jC813'.54   C95-900258-8
PZ7.B53Bo 1995

Designed by Dean Tweed
Printed in Hong Kong by the South China Printing Co. Ltd.